THE DOOMSDAY VIRUS

BY STEVE BARLOW AND STEVE SKIDMORE

ILLUSTRATED BY HARRIET BUCKLEY

COVER ILLUSTRATED BY NATHAN LUETH

Librarian Reviewer
Marci Peschke
Librarian, Dallas Independent School District
MA Education Reading Specialist, Stephen F. Austin State University
Learning Resources Endorsement, Texas Women's University

Reading Consultant
Sherry Klehr
Elementary/Middle School Educator, Edina Public Schools, MN
MA in Education, University of Minnesota

STONE ARCH BOOKS
Minneapolis   San Diego

First published in the United States in 2008
by Stone Arch Books
151 Good Counsel Drive, P.O. Box 669
Mankato, Minnesota 56002
www.stonearchbooks.com

Published by arrangement with
Barrington Stoke Ltd, Edinburgh

Library of Congress Cataloging-in-Publication Data
Barlow, Steve.
    The Doomsday Virus / by Steve Barlow and Steve Skidmore; illustrated
by Harriet Buckley.
    p. cm. — (Pathway Books)
    Summary: At age fourteen, Tim Corder is considered to be the most
dangerous criminal on the planet, but when the World Wide Web and every
computer connected to it are threatened by a virus, his expertise may be the
only hope.
    ISBN-13: 978-1-59889-871-2 (library binding)
    ISBN-10: 1-59889-871-X (library binding)
    ISBN-13: 978-1-59889-907-8 (paperback)
    ISBN-10: 1-59889-907-4 (paperback)
    [1. Computer viruses—Fiction. 2. Computer hackers—Fiction. 3. World
Wide Web—Fiction. 4. Science fiction.] I. Skidmore, Steve, 1960– II. Buckley,
Harriet, 1974– ill. III. Title.
PZ7.B2513Doo 2008
[Fic]—dc22   2007006619

Art Director: Heather Kindseth
Graphic Designer: Brann Garvey

1 2 3 4 5 6 12 11 10 09 08 07

Printed in the United States of America

TABLE OF CONTENTS

Chapter 1
The Prisoner 5

Chapter 2
The Hacker 11

Chapter 3
The Worm 19

Chapter 4
The Virus 28

Chapter 5
The Code 38

Chapter 6
The Patch 46

Chapter 7
The Lie 53

Chapter 8
The Switch 57

THE PRISONER

"Behind that door is the most dangerous criminal on this planet."

Agent Makepeace pointed at the shining steel door. Doctor Lee gave a sigh. Makepeace was a showoff, just like every other agent from the Central Security Agency (CSA).

"If he's so dangerous, then where are the guards?" asked Doctor Lee.

Agent Makepeace shook his head.

"We don't need them," he said. "No one can escape here. It's the most secure cell in the CSA."

"And how do we get in?" she asked.

The agent pointed to the wall.

"A DNA scanner. There's one inside as well," said Agent Makepeace. "You place your hand on the scanner and it checks your identity with the Central Security Agency database. If the scan doesn't recognize you, it hits you with 60,000 volts of electricity. Zap!"

The Doctor raised an eyebrow.

Agent Makepeace grinned. "It's okay, the system has been programmed to recognize your DNA. Anyway, the shock won't kill you. It's just enough to stop you from going anywhere for a while."

"And has anyone ever escaped?" asked Doctor Lee.

"No one. The system is foolproof. No two people have the same DNA."

"I know that, Agent Makepeace. I am a doctor."

"I thought you were a computer doctor," snapped Makepeace.

"The links between computers and humans are closer than you think," replied Doctor Lee. "Can we go in?"

Makepeace frowned. "I object to this meeting, Doctor. Corder is dangerous."

"The Director overruled you," said the Doctor. "We need Corder. He's the only one who can help us. I'm sure your security is fine. Even Corder can't change his DNA."

Makepeace said nothing and placed his hand against the scanner. It flashed green and the door slid open. He went through and the door closed.

Doctor Lee then placed her hand on the DNA scanner. She felt a tingling on her skin. The door opened. She stepped through and it shut behind her.

The Doctor had not expected the prison cell to be so bare. It had steel walls, a bed with white sheets and a pillow, a toilet and sink, a table and two chairs.

Sitting on one of the chairs was the most dangerous criminal on the planet. It was a thin, 14-year-old boy.

CHAPTER 2

THE HACKER

The boy looked up.

"Tim Corder?" asked Doctor Lee.

The teenager looked slowly around the room. "There doesn't seem to be anyone else here. So I must be him," he said.

"Watch what you say, Corder," said Makepeace. He raised his fist and moved forward. The doctor held up her hand to stop him.

"May I sit down?" she asked, pointing at the empty chair.

Tim smiled. "Be my guest."

Placing her black computer case and an orange file on the table, Doctor Lee sat down. Tim glanced at the file's cover.

Central Security Agency

Tim Corder –
DANGEROUS

TOP SECRET

"So, how are you, Tim?" she asked.

"I'm locked in here on my own 24/7. No visits or calls, no contact with family or friends. Not even a mouse for company," Tim said.

He nodded toward the Doctor's case.

"I don't even have a computer. How do you think I am?" asked Tim. "Anyway, I'm sure you're not here to worry about how I'm feeling. Why don't you get to the point?"

"Okay. My name is Doctor Lee. I work for a government department dealing with worldwide Internet security. We need your help."

Tim said nothing.

The Doctor opened up the orange file and began to read.

TIM CORDER. AGE 14

Dangerous computer hacker.

During his short hacking career, Tim Corder has managed to crack the top security systems of every secret service in the world: CIA, MI6, FSB, Mossad.

Tim Corder was arrested just before he was going to transfer money from the top 50 companies in the world into charity accounts.

Doctor Lee put the file down. "Very impressive, Tim."

"A real Robin Hood," sneered Agent Makepeace. Tim gave him a hard look.

"Many people might say that what Tim was doing was a good thing, Agent," said Doctor Lee.

"It was a criminal act," said Makepeace. "That's why he's in here."

Doctor Lee turned the page. "It says in your file that your partner, code-named Zeen, has never been caught." She closed the file and stared at Tim.

"You think I'm going to tell you Zeen's real name?" Tim laughed.

The Doctor shook her head. "No, and I'm not going to ask."

"So why are you here?" asked Tim.

"You're clever, Tim. Maybe even a genius. That's why you've been locked away here with no access to a computer. Someone like you is a danger to the whole planet," said Doctor Lee.

"But you could also be helpful," she continued. "We need you. There's a computer virus out there."

"There are always viruses on the Web, thousands of them," said Tim.

"This one is different," replied the Doctor. "This is the big one. The one you hackers have talked about for a long time. This is the Doomsday Virus. When it goes on the attack, the virus will destroy the Internet and every computer network on this planet."

"Sweet," said Tim. "So what's this got to do with me?"

"We think you're the only person in the world who can stop it."

CHAPTER 3

THE WORM

Tim stared at Doctor Lee. "What makes you think I can help you? Even if I wanted to?" he asked.

Makepeace pointed a finger in Tim's face. "Don't think you're the only one working on this, big shot," he snapped. "We've got real experts on the case."

Tim stared back. "But they haven't cracked it, or you wouldn't be here."

Makepeace glared and said nothing.

Tim turned to Doctor Lee.

"What if I do help you? What's in it for me?" he asked.

The Doctor glanced at Makepeace, who gave an angry nod.

"If you break the source code, we will offer you your freedom," she said.

"What?" said Tim. "I walk out of here? Just like that?"

"No," snarled Makepeace. "Not just like that! You'll be watched! If you ever try to program anything bigger than an alarm clock, you'll be back in here so fast your pants will catch on fire!"

There was a moment's silence as Tim thought about this. Then, he nodded.

"Tell me about it," he said.

The Doctor unzipped her computer case, pulled out a new laptop and switched it on. Tim's eyes flashed.

"Two days ago, the CSA received an e-mail with a warning that a worm would be released onto the Web," said Doctor Lee. "We don't know who sent it."

The Doctor turned the computer's screen to face Tim.

"This is it," she said.

Doctor Lee waited for Tim to react, but he just shrugged.

"Read it again, kid," Makepeace said. "Look at the date that the worm will be released — the fourth. That's today!"

"Is it the fourth? I lose track of time in here." Tim showed the agent his left wrist. "I don't have a watch. It was taken away."

The Doctor gave Tim a look. "It's now five o'clock. We have two hours before the worm is released."

"Is that all?" said Tim. "You'd better tell me more."

"The attachment on the e-mail was the worm itself—code-named Doomsday," Doctor Lee told him. "It wasn't a live worm, just the source code."

Tim looked puzzled.

"Nobody gives a warning that they're going to destroy the Web. They just do it. Unless this is some kind of blackmail," he said.

Makepeace shook his head. "There haven't been any demands for money."

"Then maybe it's a joke. Someone is trying to trick you," Tim said.

"We did think it might be a trick at first," said Doctor Lee. "Our experts ran tests to see how great the threat was. They found out that Doomsday will act like every worm infection on a computer.

"Like a human virus that passes from person to person, this will pass itself from computer to computer. A small piece of code will get into a computer, copy itself, then send itself to other machines."

"No problem then," said Tim. "Just write a security patch that people can put on their computers to protect them against the worm."

"Don't you think that we thought of that?" sneered Makepeace.

Doctor Lee shook her head.

"We've never seen anything like this coding before," she said. "It breaks all the rules of programming. If this worm is released into the wild, it will make all the earlier worms look like Wiggly-woo."

Makepeace frowned.

"Wiggly-woo?" he asked.

Doctor Lee gave a sigh. "It's a children's song, Makepeace. There's a worm at the bottom of my garden, and his name is Wiggly-woo."

Makepeace stared at her. "What does that have to do with our problem?"

The Doctor ignored him. "Doomsday could cause even more damage than the Slammer worm."

"The one that caused the power blackouts in America?" said Tim.

"That's top secret information," snapped Makepeace. "How do you know the blackouts were caused by the Slammer worm?"

"I just know," he replied.

"The Doomsday worm will search the Web and try to infect any of the world's four billion computers," said Doctor Lee. "Once it gets into a computer, it will turn the machine into a zombie."

After a moment, she continued, "This zombie computer will then try to infect other machines. The more computers that get infected, the more messages will be sent, and the more worms will be created.

"Doomsday has the power to grow at an amazing rate. It will double itself every two seconds."

Tim nodded. "Which will crash the whole Internet in less than ten minutes," he said.

Tim added, "Now, that is a problem."

"No," said Doctor Lee. "That's only part of the problem."

CHAPTER 4

THE VIRUS

"Let me guess," said Tim. "The worm has got a virus attached to it?"

"Correct," replied Doctor Lee. "The same day we got the Doomsday worm, a CD arrived in the mail." She reached over and tapped at the keys. Another message appeared on the computer screen.

"So when the worm hits a machine, the virus will arrive as well," said Tim. "What will it do?"

"The virus will infect the computer's hard drive," said Doctor Lee. "We ran it on a test machine that wasn't connected to any other computer. It destroyed everything."

The Doctor continued, "If this virus gets out, the program will delete stored information all over the world. And it will erase the hard drives of every computer it infects."

"It sounds like a Trojan horse to me," said Tim.

"What's a Trojan horse?" asked Agent Makepeace.

Tim rolled his eyes.

"It's a computer program," said Doctor Lee. "It pretends to be something it's not. It gets into a computer and fools the user into opening it up by pretending to be an important message or document."

"A virus can only infect a machine if it's opened," said Tim. "The computer user has to open up the virus to make it run. That's part of the challenge. A virus writer has to fool the person into opening up the program."

"Doomsday is different," Doctor Lee told him. "The coding on the worm fools the computer itself into opening the virus program. It'll get past any virus protection software. No system is safe."

"I suppose turning off the main Internet servers is out of the question?" said Tim.

Doctor Lee shook her head.

"The modern world can't exist without the Net," she said. "What happens when we turn the Web back on? Doomsday will still be there."

Tim gave a low whistle. "Wow! A double whammy! The Doomsday worm crashes the Internet, and the Doomsday Virus trashes all the information on every machine. Sweet!"

"Sweet! Is that what you think?" Makepeace exploded with anger. "What sort of sick person are you? Everything that depends on computers will fail. There'll be no cell phones. No banks. No transportation. No satellites. Without satellites to help them, oil tankers will get lost and planes will drop out of the sky!"

Makepeace jabbed a finger at Tim's chest. "That's just for starters. Power stations will shut off. No electricity, gas, or water. Without supermarket computers to order food, the shelves will be empty."

Makepeace continued shouting. "People will riot. Who'll take care of that? The army, the police, the fire fighters, and ambulance services will be unable to move. Defense systems will think they've been attacked and fire nuclear missiles, which will make other countries fire back!"

Makepeace glared at Tim, breathing hard. "Doesn't the end of the world matter to you?"

"I'm locked up in this room. Why should it?" said Tim.

Makepeace moved towards Tim.

"Back off," warned Doctor Lee. "Tim, if you break this source code and write a security patch to stop Doomsday, you'll be set free."

She pushed the computer towards him. "The worm and virus programs are in here. Will you help us?"

Tim reached for the laptop and began tapping at the keys. Doctor Lee and Makepeace looked on in silence.

Minutes passed before Tim spoke. "The virus is polymorphic."

"Oh no," whispered Doctor Lee. "Then we're finished."

CHAPTER 5

THE CODE

Makepeace stared at her. "Why are we finished, Doctor Lee?"

"A polymorphic virus means that every time the worm sends itself to another machine, it changes its code," said Doctor Lee.

"Security patches only work if they know what they're looking for. If the code is never the same, the worm will always get passed the security."

"Maybe not," said Tim. "If I can see how the code changes when it is sent to a computer, I might be able to come up with something. I'll need to connect this laptop to a network to see what happens to the code."

Makepeace let out a cry. "Connect it to the Net? No way."

Tim shrugged. "Then I can't help you. Like you said, it's the end of the world."

"Agent Makepeace!" Doctor Lee's voice was sharp. "I must remind you, the Director instructed you to offer me every cooperation. Every cooperation."

"You don't have to connect me to the Web," Tim said. "Just your internal network. You can protect it from the Web while I'm working, if you don't trust me."

"You can't connect to the Web in here," said Makepeace. "There's no line into this cell."

Doctor Lee pointed to her laptop. "This machine has wireless technology. It will connect by radio waves. All you have to do is take the CSA network offline and connect this machine to it. Time is ticking away. Do it now, Agent."

Makepeace turned his back and flipped open his phone.

As he snapped out orders, the Doctor spoke to Tim in a low voice, "Can you stop Doomsday? Really?"

"I'll give it my best shot, Doc."

Makepeace flipped his phone shut. "You have access to the internal network," he said.

The Doctor stroked the laptop's touchpad. The Central Security Agency logo flashed up on the screen. She passed the computer back to Tim.

Tim's fingers danced over the keyboard.

"I'm going to try to crack the code for the worm," he said. "That's the most important thing. Without the worm, the virus has no means of transport, so it can't spread."

A box appeared on the screen. It filled with flowing lines of code, flashing and changing so quickly that Doctor Lee was unable to read them.

Makepeace stared at the screen. "It's just numbers and symbols. How can junk like this mess up the whole Internet?"

Tim's eyes never left the screen.

"Computers work with this junk," said Tim. "Infecting someone else's machine is easy."

Makepeace gave him a nasty look. "How come?"

"People are lazy," Tim answered. "It's easy to stop viruses. You can buy software protection, but that only works on older viruses.

"There are always new viruses turning up, so you have to keep getting newer protection, but most people don't bother."

"They wouldn't need to, if punks like you didn't keep messing around with computers," Makepeace told him.

"It's human nature," said Doctor Lee. "The minute someone makes something, someone else has to work out a way to break it. Hackers see it as a game. They try to write new worms and viruses faster than companies can make security patches for them.

"That's why it's a bad idea to run a program from a source you don't know," Doctor Lee continued. "And opening any e-mail attachment can be risky."

"Even if you know the sender, you don't know whether their machine's been infected," she continued. "They may not know it has. You could let in a Trojan horse."

"Thanks for the advice." Makepeace took Doctor Lee by the arm.

He led her into a corner of the room where Tim couldn't hear them.

"What I need to know from you right now is can the kid really crack this code?" asked Makepeace.

Doctor Lee shook her head.

"I don't know. He lost me quite a while ago. He's working so fast on the computer that I can't follow him," she said.

Makepeace ground his teeth. "I don't trust him."

"We have to trust him," said Doctor Lee. "I don't know if he can stop Doomsday. I do know that if he can't, then no one can."

CHAPTER 6

THE PATCH

Time passed. Makepeace prowled around the room like a caged tiger. He loosened his tie, then unbuttoned the collar of his shirt. He checked his watch. "Only 30 minutes left."

Doctor Lee kept her eyes on the screen, trying to follow what Tim was doing as he checked and rechecked codes. Every now and then, she understood for a moment what he was doing but seconds later, Tim would lose her again.

"Fifteen minutes," Makepeace said. "You're running out of time."

"Tim?" Doctor Lee looked worried.

"I'm cool." Tim didn't look cool. He looked as if the stress was starting to get to him, but his fingers never stopped working on the laptop.

"Ten minutes." Makepeace ran his fingers through his hair. "This is going nowhere."

"Come on, Tim," muttered Doctor Lee. "Nail that worm."

"I'm working on it," he said.

There was a long silence.

Makepeace said, "Three minutes."

The codes stopped rolling across the screen. Tim looked up.

"It's done," he exclaimed. "The software patch for Doomsday is ready for release. It will kill the worm and stop the virus from getting out. All you have to do is reconnect your network to the Web right now and let it go."

"Just a minute," Makepeace said, shaking his head. "How can we trust you, Tim? It's too risky."

"What happens if we don't?" snapped Doctor Lee. "Would you rather deal with Doomsday? Give the order now!"

Makepeace spoke into his phone.

Doctor Lee snatched her computer back and clicked on the Internet browser. She gave a sigh of relief as it opened up. She looked at Tim.

Tim nodded. "Press the Send button."

Doctor Lee's finger pushed the key.

Makepeace flipped his phone shut and checked his watch. "Thirty seconds!"

The Doctor typed on the keyboard. A picture appeared on the screen.

"This shows the Web," she said. She pointed. "The lines show traffic, and the blinking dots are hubs. If the lines break and the dots go out, the worm has worked and the Net is down."

In a cracked voice, Makepeace said, "It's time. Doomsday."

Nothing happened.

Nothing continued to happen. The lines continued to glow, the hubs continued to blink.

Doctor Lee breathed, "He's done it!"

CHAPTER 8

THE LIE

Doctor Lee turned to Tim. "You did it!"

"Sure I did." Tim leaned back and placed his hands behind his head. "You said it yourself, Doc. I'm the best!"

Makepeace grunted.

Tim pointed at the Doctor's laptop.

"I'm sure your experts will be able to come up with a security update for the virus," he said. "Just in case it gets released on the Web some other way. If you have a problem, let me know."

"Thank you, Mr. Corder." Doctor Lee shut down the laptop and slipped it back into its case.

She smiled at Tim. "Can I get you anything?" she asked.

"No," snapped Agent Makepeace. "You can't."

Tim gave Doctor Lee a twisted smile. "Chill out, Doc. Anyhow, I'll be out of here soon."

"Why, yes, that's right." Doctor Lee gave Tim a half smile. "Goodbye, then."

She walked to the door and placed her hand against the DNA reader. After a few seconds, the door opened. The Doctor went out. The door closed.

Tim gave Makepeace a friendly grin.

"So, when do I check out?" Tim asked Agent Makepeace.

Makepeace returned the grin with a sneer. "You don't," he said.

Tim's face became angry. "What do you mean? You said if I cracked Doomsday, you'd let me go."

"I lied." Makepeace smiled.

Tim stared at him and said nothing.

"You fool!" snarled Makepeace. "Did you really believe the CSA would let you go, kid?"

"You've just shown why we'd be crazy to do that!" continued Makepeace. "If we let you loose, there'd soon be another virus out there, ten times worse than Doomsday. You wouldn't be stopping it. You'd be sending it! You're not going anywhere, wise guy. You'll stay in here until you rot!"

CHAPTER 8

THE SWITCH

Makepeace turned and marched to the door. He put his hand on the DNA scanner.

There was a flash. Blue lines of electricity crackled and sparkled around Makepeace. They wrapped him in a moving web of energy. The agent gave a yell. His body went stiff. His eyes stared into space.

58

The electricity field snapped off. Makepeace fell to the floor.

"Oops," said Tim. He got up from his chair and crossed the room. He bent down over Agent Makepeace.

"I know you can hear me," he said.

Makepeace said nothing. He couldn't. His eyes looked at Tim.

"I thought you might go back on your promise," said Tim. "So I had a backup plan. You were right not to trust me. You should never have let me into the CSA network.

"Of course, you had no choice. In fact, it only took me a few seconds to rewrite the codes to stop the Doomsday worm. Would you like to know what I was doing the rest of the time?"

Makepeace's eyes flashed angrily.

"I was hacking into your system," Tim went on. "I changed a few details. I told the database that my DNA code was yours and yours was mine. So when you used the scanner just now, it thought you were me, trying to escape. Zap!"

Makepeace flashed his teeth in a silent snarl.

Tim put his hand inside Makepeace's jacket and took out his cell phone. He dialed a number.

"Hi. It's Tim. The plan worked." He listened to the phone for a while. "Got you. OK. See you later."

He snapped the phone shut and grinned at Makepeace.

The agent was turning red with anger.

"You see," said Tim, "I was able to stop Doomsday because I wrote it."

Tim shrugged.

"Well, co-wrote it. With Zeen," Tim continued. "That was him on the phone, by the way. We had a plan that, if either of us were caught, the other would threaten to let loose the Doomsday worm. Zeen sent you the e-mail and the CD.

"We knew Doctor Lee's people wouldn't be able to fix it. Sooner or later you'd have to call me in. Once you'd let me into your system, I was home free."

Makepeace struggled to speak.

He managed to gasp out, "The guards . . . will . . . stop . . . you."

Tim shook his head.

"No guards," he said. "The system is foolproof, remember?"

Tim stood up. "The shock will wear off, soon. You'll be able to move again. Feel free to shout and kick the walls as much as you want. I did plenty of that when I first got here. It won't work of course. This cell is soundproof, in case you've forgotten."

Tim checked Makepeace's watch.

"Someone will bring you breakfast," He checked the time. "In 11 hours and 37 minutes. The service is always on time around here. Of course, by then I'll be long gone. Zeen bought an airline ticket for me, in a different name."

Tim winked at Makepeace. "An electronic ticket, of course."

Makepeace grunted.

Tim gave him a friendly pat. "Don't feel too bad. Tell you what, the next virus we create, we'll name it after you. The Makepeace Virus. Coming soon, to a computer near you. How'd you like that?"

Makepeace shook with rage.

"Hey, calm down." Tim said with a wink. "See you around."

He crossed the cell to the scanner, and pressed his hand against the screen. The door opened. Tim stepped through.

He walked down the long corridors of the Central Security Agency. At every locked door, his DNA was scanned.

The CSA people did not even look at
him. He couldn't be an intruder. The
system was foolproof.

Tim arrived at the last door. Outside
there were trees and grass. A flag
snapped in the breeze. Cars hummed
along the road beneath a clear blue sky.

A CSA agent was running up the steps toward the door. Tim opened it for him.

The man nodded at him, "Thanks," he said.

Tim said, "You're welcome." And he walked down the steps to freedom.

ABOUT THE AUTHOR

Steve Barlow and Steve Skidmore have more in common than just their first names. Both men grew up and live in England. They are both popular children's book writers. And they are both friends.

Today, "The Two Steves," as they're often called, write comedy and adventure stories together. They also enjoy performing at schools and libraries for kids of all ages.

ABOUT THE ILLUSTRATOR

On her ninth birthday, Harriet Buckley received a book of old comic strips. She immediately decided to become an illustrator and started to practice drawing her own comics.

Harriet's childhood dreams have come true, and today she works as an artist. She has illustrated a number of books and helped create several short animated films. She also paints large murals.

GLOSSARY

CIA (SEE EYE AY)—the letters stand for the Central Intelligence Agency. The CIA is part of the U.S. government and looks at information about suspicious people

code (KODE)—a set of instructions for a computer

computer virus (kuhm-PYOO-tur VYE-ruhss)—a computer program designed to damage or destroy information

DNA (DEE EN AY)—a molecule that makes every living thing unique. No two people have the same DNA.

FSB, MI6, Mossad (EFF ESS BEE, EM EYE SIKS, MOH-sahd)—the top security agencies in Russia, Great Britain, and Israel

hacker (HAK-ur)—a computer expert who breaks into other computer systems without permission

polymorphic (POL-ee-MOR-fik)—the ability to quickly change or become something different

Robin Hood (ROB-in HUD)—a person that robs from the rich to give to the poor

worm (WURM)—a computer program that attacks and damages computers

DISCUSSION QUESTIONS

1. Why do you think Agent Makepeace doesn't trust Tim Corder? Have you ever known someone you didn't trust? What things can a person do to gain someone else's trust?

2. Agent Makepeace agreed to let Tim go if he destroyed the Doomsday Virus. Why do you think the agent lied? In your opinion, is lying ever okay? Explain your answer.

3. At the end of the story, Tim escapes. Now that he is free, do you think he'll break into other people's computers again? Why or why not?

WRITING PROMPTS

1. In the story, Tim Corder loved being a hacker and working on his computer. Write about some of your favorite and least favorite things to do on a computer.

2. The Doomsday Virus would have destroyed all the computers in the world. What would your life be like without computers? Write about all of the things that would change in your life.

3. A sequel is a second book that continues the original story. Write your own sequel to this story. What will happen to Tim in the second book? Will he be captured? Will he create a new computer virus?

INTERNET SITES

Do you want to know more about subjects related to this book? Or are you interested in learning about other topics? Then check out FactHound, a fun, easy way to find Internet sites.

Our investigative staff has already sniffed out great sites for you!

Here's how to use FactHound:

1. Visit *www.facthound.com*

2. Select your grade level.

3. To learn more about subjects related to this book, type in the book's ISBN number: **159889871X**.

4. Click the **Fetch It** button.

FactHound will fetch the best Internet sites for you!